Friday on the Trail

Jim Bondy

PublishAmerica
Baltimore

© 2009 by Jim Bondy.
All rights reserved. No part of this book may be reproduced, stored in a retrieval system or transmitted in any form or by any means without the prior written permission of the publishers, except by a reviewer who may quote brief passages in a review to be printed in a newspaper, magazine or journal.

First printing

PublishAmerica has allowed this work to remain exactly as the author intended, verbatim, without editorial input.

ISBN: 978-1-4489-8194-6 (softcover)
ISBN: 978-1-4489-6300-3 (hardcover)

PUBLISHED BY PUBLISHAMERICA, LLLP
www.publishamerica.com
Baltimore

Printed in the United States of America

Contents

Chapter 1: How to Walk 7
Chapter 2: Waterfall and Pain 11
Chapter 3: Terra Cotta 17
Chapter 4: The Devil's Pulpit 34
Chapter 5: Packing with Pam 39
Chapter 6: Ghost Hunting 44

Chapter 1
How to Walk

    Well…it looks like I'm going to get started on this explanation of why I need to walk. Really I'm not sure why, but I've always craved hiking. I could go for miles and miles. I mean for kilometers and kilometers. Hmmm…it just doesn't roll off the tongue so well.
    When I was a young boy, (probably about 4 or 5), I used to panic my parents. I'd take a walk alone. Mind you, we lived in a good neighborhood, so there was never any real danger for my wellbeing. Anyway, I'd power-walk around the block. It was a pretty good size trek too. By the time I returned home mom was already frantically searching the neighborhood.
    "How many times do I have to go looking for you?" she'd squeal.
    Sheesh, I used to hate scaring her, but the trail was beckoning to me. I just wanted to hike.
    I guess that I'm around ten now. We moved further away from our old home on Donnelly Street. Still attending the same school but now I'm trekking a little farther. Danny, Steve and myself, (these guys I grew up with), used to walk down Sandwich street. Way down to Ojibwa Bush. We'd pack a little fry pan, lard, and eggs and traipse all through the woods until we found just the perfect clearing. I remember it like it was yesterday.

We'd brush away the leaves and pull out a little jar of Canned Heat and spark it up. Man nothing in the whole universe was as savory as those eggs, or as crisp as the water from our 'surplus store canteens' on those frosty autumn Saturday mornings.

I'm twelve or thirteen now and still living on Indian Road. Another pal, Garry and I used to go on tramps to Yachea Bush. Man did we get the crap scared out of us on one of our treks. We were walking down the old 'scrap yard' road to our destination in the bush. I wasn't supposed to go here, but you know…what the heck. Why not? Well out of one driveway, three kids appeared and followed behind us. The next house had two more of the demons joining them, yelling at us to stop. We just kept on going, picking up the pace a lot, acting as if no one was there, and hoping that if we ignored them and not respond or make eye contact, they would disappear. A little down the road another shrew got in our face and started pushing us. Needless to say, we were way outnumbered six to two and somehow got past these guys and ran and ran and ran. Did I say that we ran? I think that we just stopped. For Pete's sake…don't these kids have any parents? Don't their moms and dads know what these little creeps were up to? It seemed planned as though this was a little game. **If…**they did have any parents, their folks probably thought that the little vixens were just having some fun…throwing a scare into the wimps. Meanwhile two kids, (namely us), were probably scarred for eternity.

Well we've moved to our new house on Rosedale Ave., (a couple of block from Indian Rd), and I'm sixteen. Guess what. I still crave the trek. I need to walk. I want to walk! What is this? Now I'm into longer excursions. It's a sunny, hot Sunday afternoon. I'm now donning my 'Kung Fu' hat and cool boots, and off I go from Rosedale, down Riverside Drive, down Old Tecumseh Road, down Old Number Two. All the way to Belle River. Stay for a cool refreshing cola and head back.

There was a big cavern between seventeen and thirty, when I 'made merry' way too often. I can remember, (vaguely), when I was a teen. Every weekend, we'd find a way to get booze. My buddies would get a box of beer. God I hated beer. It was just too gross. I'd get a bottle of 'Rot Gut Whiskey'. You could mix it with pop…you know…to make it taste better. Great. Man, I'd get soooo sick. I'd have a hangover that lasted for three days. Swear it off every time, I did. Friday would come again, and sure enough. "More booze, please." I'd place my request. Holy cow...what a waste of time, money, and energy. I wish I could do that one over.

Of course, we had a rock and roll band back then. It was so cool and smack in the heat of the 'Beatle Revolution'. We knew every song, and could 'belt them out' pretty well too. The three of us had a blast! I guess that I had the most money (or best credit), because I bought most of the equipment...Drums, mics, mixer, amp, etc. We took a zillion pictures and miles of 'super eight' film, just goofing around.

Well like most of the basement bands, we slowly drifted away from it, and became somewhat average human beings. Getting half decent jobs and blowing our paychecks on girls, booze, fast cars, and poker. Man did I ever get the poker bug. I used to go around at mid-week and organize a game. A lot of the time I was broke, so I would say: "Spot me thirty bucks and I'll pay you back on 'Friday'." Hence, my nickname became 'Friday'. When I run into some of the old boys, they still call me that. If they knew me better now I would be called Friday on the Trail.

I turned it around one day. At a poker game, I lost my rifle, shotgun and rack. From that day on, I dropped poker from my itinerary, and stuck to it. Actually, I had wanted to quit for a long time, and just needed a good reason. It was an arduous task but I made it. Now I just visit the casino once a year with twenty bucks; pump it into a slot machine, then bail out. After this hit, I'm ok for another twelve months.

Have I said why I love to walk yet? You know I'm not too sure. Why is it so alluring? Anyway, at forty-two guess what job I took on. Right! Supervisor. Guess what I do most. Right! Walk. I walk and trudge and trudge and walk some more, for around nine hours straight. I'm like a cop on a beat. I walk. Hmmmmmmm.

I've got kids, you know. I guess I'm fifty or so. Do you know what I get them to do?...No?...Walk!! I bring them to the trail. It seems that we reminisce about our adventures every time we get together now. Kim and I went for a trial hike on the Chrysler Greenway. Power-walked for one and a half hours and landed in Mcgregor. It was a kind of cool spring morning. It was perfect. We could have gone forever. This was a kind of wussy trail, (old train track) but really a charming walk. The trail is totally hidden by brush and trees. We stopped for fifteen minutes at the rest area…had a juice-box each and a hit of chocolate. The jaunt back was a lot harder. It turned out that our footwear needed to be updated. Wow! This was a good opportunity for the evaluation. It was torture, but a blessing in disguise as a trek on the trail can be unforgiving.

CHAPTER 2
Waterfall and Pain

Kim and I went backpacking in the Halton Hills of the Bruce Trail. Thursday we drove up. We landed there close to dusk hoping we could find a spot to park. Man we searched up and down the roads figuring that surely some little nitch would pop up. No dice, and now it's starting to get late. It'll be dark soon. What are we going to do, sleep in the car? Finally, we embarked on a golf course and asked at the pro shop, where we could store our car for a couple of days to hike the 'Bruce'. He advised us that the trail followed right along the top of the property, and we could park in the lot for the 3 days for $15.

"Just park right over there," he gestured, pointing about 10 meters to the right. "You can set your tent up off of the third fairway, just over by the bush," he said.

Holy cow. Thank God. We thought that we were goners. Didn't know what to do. This could have been a real crappy kickoff to already a short weekend. The clearing that we picked was perfect. We pitched our tent smack on the edge of the woods. It had a roiling brook trailing right along us, which doubled as a fridge for our six-pack of beer. A small arch spanned the stream. This made for a comfortable roost to stop, enjoy the enticing view, and recoup the days' journey.

We got up early, strapped our backpacks on and hit the trail, heading North from '6th line' road. The path starts out here with steps carved right out of the rock face. Man, it's awesome already but right off the bat, we're heading straight up. I can already feel the straps tugging hard on my shoulders. The gravitational pull was quite evident, but who cares? This is what it's all about. Probably should have accomplished a little more training…Nah!

We walked along the top of the escarpment. The overwhelming terrain, with dropped cliffs gouging the landscape was truly astonishing. Gazing down at the tops of the magnificent, stately Oaks and Pines sent rushes up your whole body. The stunning elegance was breathtaking. Their sole purpose to provide life-giving oxygen seems small in comparison to the vastness of their troops. The only dilemma was the lack of water here. We had to ration all along this part of the journey.

At one point, we came across a quarry. The trail had an expansion bridge with a see-through mesh walkway, navigating high over the road

"I'm not going over that," I queried.

"Over what?" Kim asked.

"Over that." I repeated

Kim gave me a sideward glance. "You're afraid of going over the bridge?"

"Who me? No. I think that I'll head back and sit in the car until you're done your hike. Ok?" I joked.

"Dad!"

"What?" I think that I led this on for long enough.

"Lets go," Kim insisted.

"Ok. Come on what are you waiting for." I said as I started to traverse the span.

"Arrrrrg. I should throw you over the edge," Kim growled.

"I'm a bad boy," I gleamed.

This was a choice area to take a few snapshots and rest for a while. We quartered an orange to help quench our thirst then onward we prodded. You really need to be in good physical condition to be here especially carting all of this weight. The path is all ups and downs. Seems like it's more ups than downs!

FRIDAY ON THE TRAIL

We followed this part of the trail till about lunchtime. We decided to make a peanut butter and jam sandwich, so I opened my pack where we kept the grub. One look was all it took to decide that we needed more secure containers. The jam lid popped open. Nice, gooey jelly everywhere, and absolutely no spare water to clean it up. It seemed to work it's way to every piece of anything in the compartment. This yuck haunted us for the rest of the day.

Next we arrived at the junction joining the Bruce Trail to the side trail that led to the Hilton Falls. We decided to take this route. It seemed to be at a lower elevation and the trail was damp looking. We found some water here. It was such a welcome sight. We didn't want to devour all of our hydrating snacks and juice boxes right off. I filled the reservoirs in our backpacks using my handy dandy purifier. You could draw moisture out of a boot print in the mud and drink it right down. I don't know how we would have survived without it. It was the most critical hundred bucks that I've spent in my life. At least that's how it seemed at the time.

We snaked along the trodden path for hours on end. The straps of the backpacks were like knives, cutting deep into our shoulders. We were overheated and exhausted. For about the last hour we envisioned that we were coming to our destination just around the every crook. Instead we just found more trail. Now, we could hear thunder in the distance. We didn't pay much attention to it but soon altered our way of thinking when it started to pour. It felt refreshing. We were hot and getting drenched. That was nice…Thanks God, but now we have to get our ponchos out. These ponchos were not cheap. Kim paid…I'll bet…two dollars and fifty cents each for them. Well…they did do the trick but there's no way that they would have carried us through another downpour. The main objective though was to keep our sleeping bags dry, and they served us well for that purpose.

We must have been a pitiful sight, perched on the boulders praying for the monsoon to stop, eating another big orange and nutritional bar, in an effort to give us the strength to go on. It wouldn't have been so bad, but along with the rain, (which didn't bother us), the trail was flooded. There was nowhere to walk save the puddles. Once my feet got soaked, I died.

Man, how do you protect yourself against this? Neoprene socks! Next trip we'll be prepared.

We hiked forever…in and out of the bush following 'blue'. Sometimes on the path, then back into the undergrowth. These side trails are brutal but we must follow the blue hash marks. There was a break in the rain, and we just happened to see a welcoming pond just off the passage. We were completely exhausted. We had ambled on the trail for 9.5 hours of grueling climbing and treking.

"What do you think? Should we keep on going to try to make it to the falls?" I asked.

"I don't know. What do you think?" Kim totally exhausted by now.

I was no better. We kept walking for about twenty steps. Stopped. Took about ten more steps. Stopped.

"We should camp now," I weakly said. "What about that little pond just right there," I pointed back.

"You think?" Kim asked.

"Yea, how about you?" I said, taking a few more steps.

We kept walking down the path for about two minutes and the blue hash mark wanted to turn us back into the heavy growth. This would have guaranteed almost impassable, rough terrain.

We just looked at each other. "No way." We chanted in unison.

"Lets take the campsite. There's absolutely no way we can go back into the bush. Just look at it. It's the perfect spot," Kim said.

"You don't have to convince me. Lets go," I beckoned.

It was beautiful. The rain stopped momentarily just prior to our arrival. We decided to set up the tent pronto in case the rain returned. No sooner did we place our gear into it, we could hear the drops pounding on the walls. Fortunately we were ahead of the game. A little later we created a gratifying dinner, cleaned up and just relaxed. The rain stopped. A muskrat family frolicking in the pond provided us with outstanding entertainment. The rushing water provided us with a cooler for our left over beers. The panoramic spectacle of the escarpment, pond and waterfall provided an attractive backdrop for pictures. A huge momma turtle was laying eggs in the comforting warm sand just outside of our campsite. We really lucked out; especially Kim when the turtle lunged forward and nearly chomped her finger. There was something soothing about this spot that totally relaxed us. Later that evening we hit the sack hard. I don't think that I've ever been as sore, as I was that night in the tent. I couldn't move.

At the break of dawn we got all of our morning duties complete, packed up and headed straight down the path for the falls. We would have never made it if we had tried last night. We would surely have been hopelessly lost in the dark, and probably have gotten a sprained ankle in the mix.

Some hiker that we ran into on the trail informed us not to expect much of the falls.

"It's not much more that a tap running," he said.

We didn't care. We were almost there.

"Hey, even if it isn't that great; so what," I said

Kim whole heartily agreed. It took us about two hours to get there. You wouldn't have believed it. They were awesome and probably around three stories high, with a raging current, cascading off of the cliff. We were able to go down to the base and stand almost behind them, but were slightly apprehensive since we had our 'going home' clothes on. We remained here for some time, crossed the stream by the bridge, and appreciated some spectacular views from the other side.

Reluctantly after this bit of heaven we went to the Hilton Falls conservation center where we enjoyed the first drink of something cold, (Cola), that wasn't sucked out of a brook and an ice cream bar that was well worth the four dollars that they gouged us for. After a short walk down the dusty roadway, we scaled the 'climb-over' to get back on the trail. I thought that we were quite close to the golf club but we had to make our way back to the top of the escarpment. This was some really, really steep hike. We had to stop and rest half way up…Twice, (figure that one out). Landed back at the golf course around noon or so. There were golfers everywhere. We felt a little uncomfortable with our tent pitched on the edge of the third fairway. Every now and then we could hear some golfer shout "Four!," so we packed up all of our gear, went to the clubhouse patio, had 2 beers (COLD), paid our fifteen bucks for parking and headed back; home sweet home.

Have I ever mentioned that I like to walk? Love it. Star wars…outer space anything…Love it. Sword fighting, swashbuckling, three musketeers, knights of the round-table, anything medieval, I fall over backwards for. It's a guy thing…On the other hand, has it something to do with a mysterious past life?

"En guard; eh?" Oops. At least twice a year we go to a medieval dinner show. It's awesome. In the coliseum, each row of seats have banquet style benches for food. A myriad of waiters and waitresses that instruct you to call them serfs and wenches, prowl their areas, while you watch the show. It's great…with gladiators…a king and queen, villain, serfs, and more. There are jousting competitions, and many other ancient arts of display and feats of strength, all encompassed in a really wonderful story.

Chapter 3
Terra Cotta

My son, Jeff and I made it to the Bruce Trail Thursday afternoon. We drove up the Terra Cotta Conservation area. Nobody around. My map showed the Trail started here, but there were a bunch of small conservation trails converging in this area and none of them were marked as 'The Bruce Trail'. We figured out which path seemed to be the best candidate and took it, but it didn't look right. As we were walking along, the trail kind of disappeared into the undergrowth. Usually it is child's play to follow. We found an old stake rotted away at the edge of the fence that was probably part of a support for a 'walkover' at one time. We followed the six-foot chain link until we found a gate with a loose bit of the mesh at the bottom. We figured what the heck else can we do? Jeff pulled up on the fence for me and the packs to squeeze under, and I provided the same service in return. We then walked up the deserted wagon path until we figured the trail started again. We hoped that we were right but the critical white hash marks were painted over brown. We followed it anyway as we didn't know where else to go. We walked a good distance, all the while following the painted over hash marks. This was very disturbing because the trail could and likely would, just end and we'd have to turn back and go to (who knows where). Finally there it was. We met up with the new path, well marked with the paint strips that were so necessary. I still don't know where it came from or how we chanced upon it but obviously someone was watching over us.

We headed North along the trail. The scenery was plentiful, but the absence of water was overwhelming. You have to land it wherever it shows up. We found a trickling fresh mountain stream only a couple of inches wide where we cooled off and loaded up on the priceless liquid. It seemed to come from nowhere and disappeared into a rocky crevasse, but with a little patience and ingenuity we made it work for us. While we were stopped, Jeff noticed that our tent was shifted on my backpack and swinging a bit. This is the scourge of a backpacker. If something is not secure, the object fights you. When you sway right it swings left. I needed to secure it better, so I got an extra strap from him to bind it up tight. Big dilemma: my loop wouldn't take the strain and broke. I hope that that is the only thing that goes. Actually, it was a blessing in disguise because now we were stopped and I was able to lash it off properly. You've got to have a stable pack, or die.

We ended up finding a nice flat clearing right near the north junction of the Rockside 'side trail'. We ran into the purveyor of this part of the trail. He was a sixty-something year old with such a spring in his step. He was no stranger to the 'Bruce'. His small backpack sported a water bottle, some pruning shears, and a bow saw. We asked if any water could be acquired nearby. He pondered for a minute.

"Nope," he said, "all of the streams done dried up crossing the trail 'round here. Now less you want to walk a piece. You can make your way on down to the Credit River. Lots o' water there."

The atmosphere was starting to get that twilight glow. We were beat and not really sure how far it was to the River. Our water rations were still adequate to pull us through the night and breakfast. We looked at each other momentarily

"You know I think that we'll just camp right here. Thanks a bunch for the info," Jeff said.

"Yep. Take care." Was all the 'Keeper' said; and off he went. Disappeared from sight, almost like magic.

We pitched our home, and got dinner going but there was something that was creeping me out. It seemed like every time I looked over my shoulder there was an outline of something disappearing into the bush. I couldn't quite focus on it. Jeff was experiencing the same thing.

Just to make the excursion memorable, my instant coffee container exploded and mixed with the sweat from my juice box. Everything had sticky, partially hardened coffee grounds adhering to it. I mean everything: our stove, cutlery, propane, apple, plates, you name it. Guess what. No spare water to clean it up, so this made my backpack smell really good. Every animal down-wind was surely keeping a watchful eye on us. Why is it that on every expedition I've got to slime something. It was jam on my last trip. Oh well. By the time that we devoured the stew, nightfall was upon us. Man, were we glad that we didn't keep on going. After dinner, we took to the trail for a short walk, (without our packs). This sure felt light. We went up the trail a bit to see where it would bring us. We wouldn't have made it to the stream by a long shot. By the way, we never did find out what seemed to be slipping into the bush. It must have been the outline of an old rotting tree that we met in the distance

Well rested, fed and ready for anything, we moved out at the early hour of dawn, (whatever hour that is) and trekked all morning. After lunch the trail led to some road trudging with no provisions for cover from the sun. We baked. The 'cold milk' trucks that kept zooming by us didn't help since we were still desperately conserving our water. We finally slipped back into the bush early on, into the Caledon Hills section. A welcome sight it was too. It was comforting to get under the protection of the blanketing shade, even though it was extremely jagged terrain and was called the Credit Stone side trail. After a while trekking we found a gorgeous brook about 1 foot wide dawdling along right under a narrow footbridge. This was truly a gift. We washed our dishes from last nights supper, stripped down as much as we dared, (there are other hikers possibly nearby), and cleaned up before the flies found us. Next, we had to take every item out, (piece by piece), from my backpack and wash off the stiffened coffee goop, which had partially turned to concrete by now. Well we got everything back into the packs, nice and clean and organized, (as usual), all ready to rock. I grab my pack as usual to heave it over my shoulder, and just as I was hoisting it up my main shoulder strap made this huge ripping sound, that tore through my heart. I couldn't believe it. The stitching broke on half of the length of the seam, but the remainder was still holding strong. If it had torn all of the way life would have been hell. We push ourselves to the edge, with perfectly good working gear. I couldn't have imagined lugging forty-five pounds for the remainder of the trip with only one strap. Why is my pack self-destructing?

Refreshed we hit the trail north to the Chinguacousy road. This led to the deserted train track that was the turning point to start to make the loop. We took this back to the sweltering Boston Mills road again, better equipped this time with water to spare. This will lead us to the 'Rockside' side trail that was a pretty nice path. It led us all the way to the Credit River which was an overly populated area. We were kind of looking for just the right campsite. This would have been it if it weren't for the busyness of the area. Homey little cottages lined the river except right where we were. Traffic was nonstop. This wasn't what it was all about as far as we were concerned. Keep going. We put our feet in the water for a while, until the school of huge crayfish chased us out. We took a much-needed break and carried on with our quest for the perfect site. From here, we got onto the Terra Cotta side trail, back in the wilderness. We pushed on and on. Lots of ups and downs. It was the most beautiful part of the trip so far, but it was difficult. We were joking saying wouldn't it be awesome to just keep going right to the truck and camping out in Jeff's backyard. A nice glass of cold milk and a bowl of ice cream. It was hard to shake this thought, especially since it wasn't out of the realm of possibility.

"Do you want to?" I asked.

Jeff reluctantly replied, "No way. We can't wimp out now…Why do you want to?"

"No," I didn't feel sure when I said this.

"Are you sure? I could really go for a cold glass of milk," Jeff queried.

Well the conversation went back and forth for a while until we put the kibosh on even the mention of milk or ice cream.

It was getting around supper time, and Jeff again was saying, "Boy wouldn't it be nice to find just the perfect campsite with a bridge crossing a little stream?" I think that he figured, if he said this enough times it would come true.

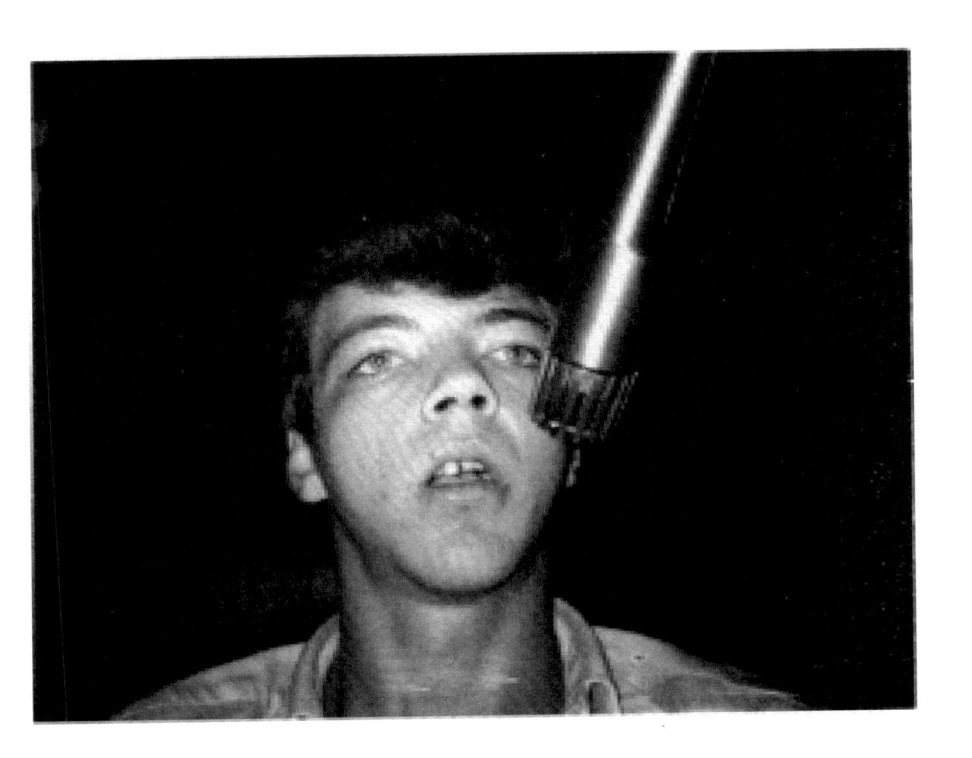

"Me when I was in the rock band"

"Just a tap running?"

"Just part of the...trail?"

"Finally lounging. It feels so good!"

"Not your regular walk in the park."

"Can you smell those flap-jacks?"

"Going? Nah…we're staying!"

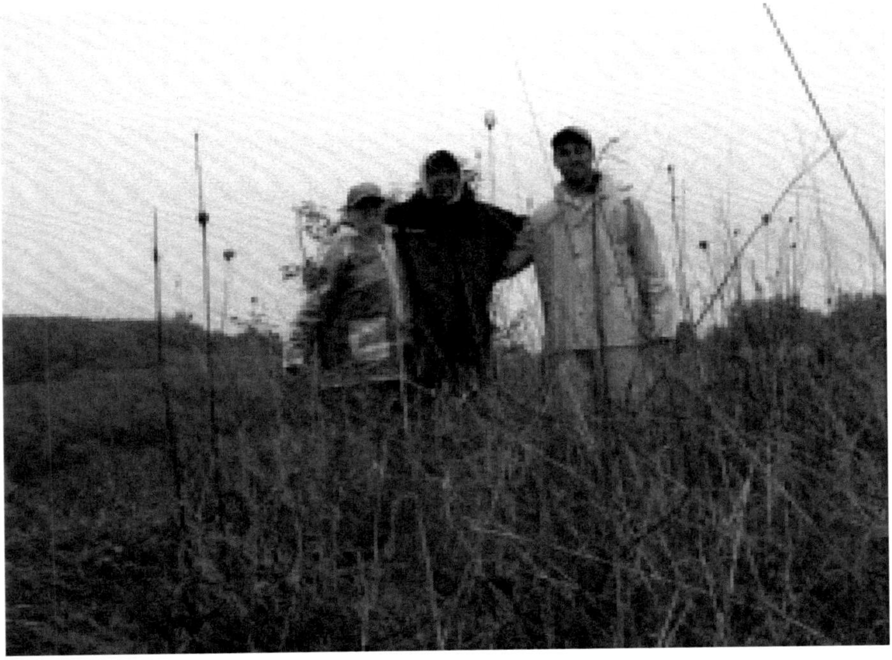

"Just walk up those steps there."

"Piece of cake"

"The family that walks together…"

"Go git em Charlie…Hey ohh!"

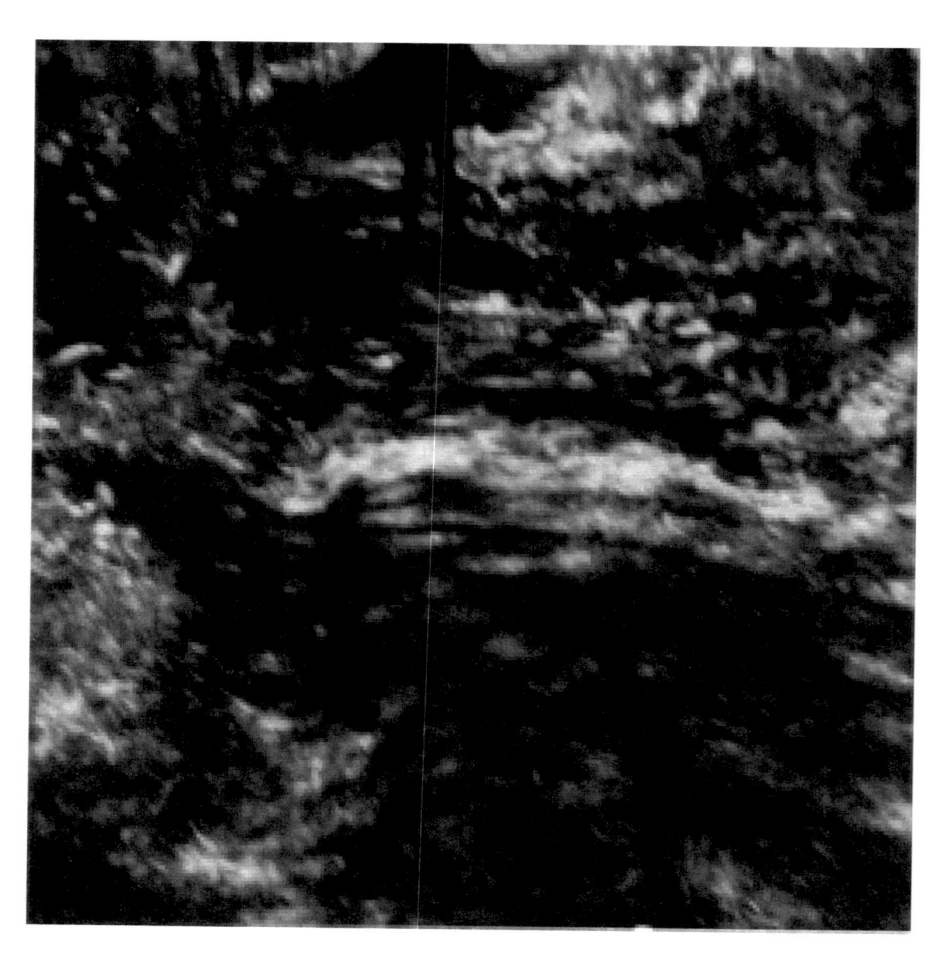

"Doesn't get any harder that this!"

FRIDAY ON THE TRAIL

It was unbelievable ten minutes later we stumbled across the perfect spot. I'll never forget it. There was a nice flat area for the tent, with a good cooking spot in front. The shallow stream was clear and running fast. It was about ten feet wide and wound its way through the bush. The old rustic bridge supplied beautiful scenery and a superior place to just sit wasting time throwing sticks into the stream, watching the caterpillar feast on the oak leaf…You know…the really important stuff. We just stayed here all morning totally relaxing. Doing pretty well nothing at all. We took our time and embraced the time on our hands. Slowly we got the ball rolling little by little. Shaved, took the tent down, loaded our packs, purified some water and just took a good look around. You wouldn't even have known anyone had been there. Off we went. We thought that the truck was near, but we were dead wrong. We walked and walked. Never mind ups and downs. It seemed to be all ups. The views were exemplary though which helped quell our exhaustion. We ended up back at the truck by about 1:00 pm. What a beautiful sight it was.

Man. What drives us to such torture? When we go, it seems like no one or nothing else exists. As soon as we got back, we were planning our next backpacking adventure. It looks like it's going to be the 'Devils Pulpit'. We just can't wait. The only problem that I can foresee is the lack of available water…AGAIN! My topo doesn't show many rivers, streams or brooks and it's been so dry lately, most of them will be parched. We'll have to pack in a lot of moisture to keep us hydrated, but it shouldn't be too bad. All three of us are going this time, and we can more equally share the extra weight.

Chapter 4
The Devil's Pulpit

The first thing that comes to memory is the site that we set up our tent on the first night. It was not too far off of the path up on top of a grassy knoll. It was raining profusely that day, but we had storm gear and were wearing it. We set up our shelter in record time so nothing would get too soaked. My rain gear was from a very reputable company and I paid dearly for it but it didn't breathe well. I was wetter wearing it, than if I hadn't. Jeff had some waterproof jacket and pants that worked out very well for him. He was used to this kind of thing because he works outdoors in construction. Kim bought a brand new clear water suit that she paid $5.99 for and it proved to be worth exactly that. It had been pouring a lot. When we got into the tent we were removing our wet rain gear. Kim slipped hers off and just stepped out for a second to get something. Jeff thought that he would help out and he grabbed Kim's rain pants and flipped them (as you would a bed sheet) to shake off some of the water. As they snapped, (from Jeffs efforts), the 2 legs just ripped right off. Flew right to the other side of the tent. We roared. I thought that I was going to die. We never laughed so hard. Kim came in just at this time.

"What's so funny?"

Jeff was laughing so hard. "Look what happened to your pants! I just flipped them to get the water off and the legs ripped right off…right on the seam. Honest I just flipped them." I was rolling on the floor.

"Oh my god." Kim responded in horror. "What am I going to do?"

Jeff was still reeling. "Don't worry Kim I'll fix it with duct tape."

"It'll never work." She squealed. Still trying not to laugh…but loosing the battle.

"Sure it will." Jeff said as he started drying the material still laughing uncontrollably. By this time Kim was laughing too.

After a couple of hours Jeff was done. He did a fantastic job. Actually it lasted for the rest of the venture.

While Jeff and Kim were starting to make breakfast I decided to go to the pond and fetch some water, so off I went. It was probably about one hundred feet downhill. Once at the pond I pulled out my purifier pump and started yanking water into my collapsible jug. The filter must be getting a little plugged. I was dead after only pumping the gallon full. I think that we'll start taking turns as we had a lot more to go before this trip was over. The rain turned into an insignificant drizzle, and being daybreak we started to move out. The terrain was rough and the trail was not too well marked. Often we were wondering if we were on it at all.

"I haven't seen a hash mark in a while." I said with a little nervousness. "Think we're on the path? It looks like it goes off that way." Pointing left.

"BLUE!" Jeff called out. Finally off to the right in the distance you could see a blue hash mark painted on a tree. This is the way that trails are marked to keep you on track. Both sides of the tree have the 6-inch by 2-inch line painted at eye level. Usually just as the last one that you see goes out of sight, you can spot the next one. This holds true if you're on the main trail, and the hash marks are white. On side trails the marks are blue, often too far apart for comfort, and the path is not well kept. One could easily take a wrong turn and be hopelessly lost.

Onward we go. The scenery is breath taking. It's a hard trek but well worth the effort.

"Blue…thank god"! Besides, if we trained harder it would be a less demanding 'go'. Whatever! We were encompassed by marsh. The trail was only slightly elevated. Can't resist getting a soaker. The terrain on these side trails really get choppy.

"Arggh." Jeff pulled his foot out of the pungent bog.

"This place stinks. I'm gonna puke." Kim was disgusted

"That's just nature making fertilizer." Jeff joked

"How can you be in such a good mood? You just stepped in it. Uhhh you stink."

"Keeps the flies off of my face."

The trail is pulling us uphill now. It's getting hard to follow again. Some pretty big boulders to climb over. Gotta love those back trails. It looks like it veers of to the right yet the hash mark is straight ahead. Sometimes you have to improvise, but you don't really want to go off of the marked path. It's easy to get side tracked…which wouldn't be so bad if you didn't have any deadline, but…You know the "W" word that comes every Monday. Hmmmm.

"Blue"! Kim noticed off to the right in the distance. "Finally. Sheesh"!

Going through the bush and out of nowhere the path leads to the base of a cliff.

"Well…it just stops dead here." I was stumped.

"Over here…in the bushes. Look." Kim pointed up.

Sure enough there were steps carved in to the side of the mountain. A rope was lagged to the face to hopefully help you from miserably falling to your death.

"We need to go up this path." Jeff said

"What path?" I was not too keen on heights.

"Up the steps!" Jeff said as he started climbing.

These steps were not what you might call safe. None of them were the same size or height. One would be 6 inches, and the next one was about one and a half feet tall and about seven inches wide. No wonder they called this the path to the Devils Pulpit.

"Oh my god!" Kim wasn't too keen on this either. "Jeff…are you sure?"

About half way up we spotted it. Hanging precariously, there was a ledge protruding out of the side of the cliff.

"How in the hell are we going to get to that?" I was looking off to the right, and there it was, about twenty feet from the steps.

"We have to keep going to the summit and then come straight down to the ledge. That's how it reads in the book." Jeff was determined. He was our inspiration.

Sure enough there was another rope lagged to the rock leading down from the top of the cliff. We all made the journey to the ledge. Once on the ledge the only thing there to protect us from cascading down the three hundred foot rock strewn chasm was annother huge rope tripled up as a railing that bridged the face of the pulpit.

Kim gasped. "This is the most beautiful view that I've ever seen. Not even in books."

She was right. The landscape…the mountains…the sheer drop to the rocks. There was no equal. How can you replicate actually being there? Television…even 3D can't make you understand the true meaning of being at a place like this. We stayed here for such a long time.

Well all good things need to just live in our memory. We must move on. We'll have to make camp before dusk. Back down the cliff, (creepier than going up), we went. After this endeavor, we dreaded trekking all of the way down the mountain just to climb back up the other side of the chasm. In the distance Jeff spotted a train trestle bridging the deep crevasse.

"Hey do you guys want to save a lot of climbing"? Jeff queried. "Look over there…looks like a bridge or something."

"You know that would really save our legs. Lets go take a look at it. What do you think Kim?" I said.

"Hey I'm all for that." Kim replied.

So off we went. It was around a half kilometer away through some pretty rough topography. We had to make our own path through the brush, but it was a lot better that the long trek down to the rushing river, then spanning it and climbing our way back up the other side. When we got to the trestle there were signs warning us to not trespass, but the temptation was overwhelming. There were workers from the train company doing some repairs near the beginning of the traverse. We asked them if they knew if there would be a train coming soon. This darn thing was narrow. It was only wide enough for the tracks and about a foot on each side...and that was it! There would be nowhere to go except down.

"No no. Don't worry. Won't no train be on dis trak today. Go head don' worry." A couple of them chanted.

Wow this was great. No possibility of trains and a great shortcut to boot. We commenced going across the bridge. Life is good. Then the ground disappeared from under the tracks. We had to leap from railroad tie to railroad tie for the whole length of the chasm. If we misjudged, it looked like a person could probably fall through the void between the ties. Kim and I were not the greatest with unsafe heights and were drawing from our full concentration trying to keep our composure. The void was probably about 20 stories deep with a hastily speeding river at its base, to help amplify the phobic dilemma.

"Oh my god...Oh crap...Oh...Oh boy...Oh boy." Every vault to each rung was an adventure. Our hearts were racing. Our adrenalin flowing. Kim and I heard a train whistle when we were half way across. Maybe it was our father / daughter imagination connection, because no train appeared. I wouldn't be alive to tell this story if it had. There had to be two hundred of these ties to land on. Every jump was as heart stopping as the last. So here's Jeff...just jumping and talking away. Mostly jumping two at a time. Not a care in the world. Not really concentrating on where he was going to land. Sometimes looking back to us to chatter away about anything and everything, truly oblivious to the danger. We heard him talking but couldn't find a breath to utter a single word. We starred straight ahead at the next landing site that we had to make, ensuring that hopefully from some freak of nature we wouldn't plunge to our imminent death. This part of the journey seemed to last for ever, then as we approached the other side of the canyon the ground rose back up under us. Sure was a stressful workout but we were still alive...not dead...not floating face down through the rapids on our path to see Saint Peter...who I'm sure would scold us for being so dumb.

CHAPTER 5
Packing with Pam

I snuck in that last trip just days before my foot surgery, and now, have to stay off of it till Christmas. I guess that I needed a break from work anyway.

Well it's three weeks after the surgery, and I'm going stir-crazy. I don't need the painkillers any longer, so now my swaying willow tree isn't the epicenter of my life anymore. I'm getting restless. I perch on my deck for a while, then hobble over to my pond and count the fish, then somehow crutch it to the 'far-back' patio for an hour, then surf the Internet for a couple hours…and so on and so on. Try doing this for days on end. A person might think that it would be heaven, (and it is), but after a short while, I've gotta go! This also gave me plenty of time to lose my money on the stock market. I must be crazy. Thanks to the Gold Mine Scandal of the century, I get to retire later then I had planned. Oh well…

My boss, Mark Z (being the nice guy that he is), is still paying my salary while I'm off, so I called him and said. "Give me something to do. I'm going nuts."

He arranged for someone to come way our in the countryside to bring me in for a couple of hours each day, then drive me home. Lots better! It also provided me time to do the more enjoyable things; like write this book; read my adventure magazines (cover to cover); and spend quality time with my favorite wife Pam.

Meet Pam, (the nicest person that ever was. Even nicer than Mark). My goal is to get her backpacking with me. We used to go camping feverously when the kids were still kids and at home. We loved it. Every long weekend; every vacation off we'd go from one end of Ontario to the other. There was nothing like it. All of the culinary treats: breakfast, coffee, and supper, were produced smack on the open fire. We used to haunt the family type campgrounds because they were spotless with nicely scrubbed showers, sinks and toilets. The owners were always friendly and courteous. Not like some of the Provincial Potties that you had to bathe with half of the spider population.

Anyway, Pam's biggest complaint was that 'square inch' where the two zippers met. Half of the time Kim or Jeff, would leave it cracked. I don't take any blame here because I am telling this story and it's my book.

"Snakes will get in," she complained. "What if a raccoon gets his paw in there and rips it open? Arrgghhh. One of these days we have to get a camper."

Well some time went by and lots more camping trips too, but as time passed we acquired a small popup camper. Everybody was happy.

Pam said. "Well that's it. You'll never get me into a tent again. I love this. NO bugs, or snakes. Raccoons can't get in. Nope. No more tents for me."

Sheesh have I got my work cut out for me. How can I convince my sweetie, that if we buy a good tupik there won't be any gaps for snakes to sneak in. I've got to make sure that she understands that raccoons won't go into a tent, (I hope...or will they), if we don't have food in there.

"All that we have to do is hang our food from a tree limb away from our campsite," I explained.

"Hang our food?" She queried.

"Yea," I said. "That way the raccoons and bears can't get to it."

"Bears! What bears?" She enquired with that sly glance.

"You know...The kind that poops in the woods." This was my desperate attempt at trying to make them look innocent.

"That's all we need. We'll be fast asleep while some grisly bear is jumping up and down, trying to reach our food; landing up against our tent; snorting and growling. Now he's bummed, because he can't reach our food; and smells us!" Pam rambled.

I joked, "Make sure you shower"

I came back. "Besides there aren't any grislys around here."

"Whatever!" She rolled her eyes.

I could see that her imagination was running amuck, and nothing was going to slow her rage. "Well black-bears are much less aggressive. They probably won't come anywhere near us."

"You're right," she said. "They aren't coming any closer to me than the TV screen."

This is, as challenging as I expected. Hmmmmmmm. I need a new approach. Gotta keep thinking.

Well the second phase of my foot healing process just came to pass. The good surgeon removed that God-awful pin that's been forcing my toe to behave. I can move again. Maybe I can walk a little. "OUCH!" Oops. I guess, not yet.

Well with the help of a crutch or two, I've been slowly coming around. I can even bend it some, again.

"I can drive!" I cheered. This is great. I don't have to bother my pals at work to make the twice-daily journey, out to the boonies to pick me up. Before you know it, I'll be able to go hiking again. "Three hundred feet up…two hundred feet down. Over the boulders…across the stream. Soaker? No problem. Pouring rain…HA! Bring it on!!" We'll chant. "Throw it at us!" Man, I wish that I had thought like this when I was twenty-something. Oh well, too late now.

Well we've done it. It can at least be called a darn good start. Pam and I went for a day-hike at Point Pelee Provincial Park. It was awesome. I bought a new backpack, because if you recall, at the Terra Cotta trip my old pack was falling apart. Well this pack has a lifetime guarantee. I finally got to try it out and it's great. I hardly knew that I had it on. Of course I'm training on the 'DeLaurier trail', which is not the most strenuous trek I've been on. We didn't know that it was going to be so scenic. It reminded me of the 'Bruce' at spots, as it wound its way over streams, and through marshes. Pam kept up very well for her first time on the trail. The air was crisp with a slight dusting of snow, falling straight down. Not a breath of wind to discomfort us. The snowflakes turned into the gentlest of snow pellets, increasing in density. It was beautiful. The calmness...the silence was enchanting. We did the whole trail with this scene. Just as we were ending our journey, the angry winds became turbulent and increased in velocity. Suddenly we had near blizzard conditions. It was hard to tell that this is the most Southern point of Canada. The snow started to thicken. We barely made it to the parking lot due to the lack of visibility. We found our way to the car. I removed my backpack and off we went to another trail in the park. The only problem that I encountered was the fact that snow collected between my pack and my neck. I'll have to check out what to do about this. Maybe there is no real good answer, or I need better waterproofing. I don't know. I'll go on the net and chat with other hikers that are used to winter treks.

Next we pulled up to the trail that goes to the point. Pam and I bundled up tight and fought the blizzard conditions to get to the West Beach area. It was unbelievable. The waves were enormous...crashing to the pristine beachhead. If we were to hike here we would have had to go north first, against the gale-force winds, then return with the wind at our backs. The snow was incredible. We decided to get into the underbrush, where we had better odds against Mother Nature. We weren't attempting to prove anything today, we just wanted to be out, and enjoy the scenery. We got back to the car and drove to the center where we took a needed pee break and look-around.

We took a look out the back, and found another trail that steered out into the bush. We figured that it was a short trail, so I didn't bring my pack. Off we went. The snow was slightly effervescent here. We walked forever. The swamps surrounded us. Hauntingly beautiful with its felled trees, huge tangling vines. A Tanager flitters right by us...landed on a sleeping hollow log. What a wonderful contrast. We're still treking. A long hour had passed, and there's still no sign of the end. Winding right and left...over bridges and through brush. I was beginning to wonder if we missed a marker leading us back to the starting point. Darkness was falling. We're still going. It's getting colder now. We weren't really prepared for this. I wish that I had my pack on. There was a blanket in it that would have helped keep us toasty. The trail displayed some hints that we had been there before. Surely it was my imagination. Pam didn't seem to be apprehensive at all, so I didn't concern her with my doubts. She kept up with her naturally cheerful chatter that she is great at. She trusts that I know exactly what's going on and that's that.

Round the next bend we go. The snow is getting heavier. Ahhhh…a marker. "Turn right for 200 m to the center," it said.

Oh yeah! No problem. It couldn't have been a nicer sight. "We can do this," I said.

Pam replied, "Do what?"

"Never mind," I replied. "The car isn't too far up the trail."

"Yeah that's what the marker showed," Pam said confidently.

"Yup"

We got to the car and sparked up the heater and in no time we warmed up. It's a good thing that Pam thought that I had everything under control. Maybe I still have a fair shake at getting her on the wilderness trails. Keep your fingers crossed.

Chapter 6
Ghost Hunting

I'll never forget the long weekend that Charlie, Tabernac (Jerry), and myself went ghost hunting. Every May 24 weekend we would go up to Charlies home town for our "Fishing Trip." My best friend 'Charlie' was from that area. He knew that countryside like the back of his hand. The colorful tales that he used to belt out were purely entertaining. We'd snake through the bush, followed broken down train tracks that had been abandoned for decades. He knew of streams that were only a couple feet wide and about as deep, but had trout as long as your forearm. He could catch them too! He just knew where to throw in his line.

"Just throw your line in under that grassy bluff." Charlie was a natural at it. So I'd cast under the thickets and kind of land in the spot, but didn't get a nibble. Tabernac did the same with equal results.

"Too bad." He snickered, and threw in his line at the next spot. "Yes!" he cheered. Sure enough, a nice rainbow.

"Arrrghhh." We echoed. "Maybe if the black flies weren't so thick…Look it's snowing! Charlie!

"Ahhh you guys are just wimps. Just forget about the black flies. The more that you swat them away, the more you sweat, the more they like you. Just kind of wipe them off you…and that's not snow…it's just early spring fluff."

"Bull." Tabernac laughed. "That's snow. It's freezing"

"Naaaah. Come on you guys. Toughen up." Charlie teased.

We knew what we were getting into. Every year it was the carbon copy of the last, and we were bound to it…destined to repeat the past. To aid us in our acceptance of the inevitable we would pack up as much of the frosty brew as we could carry, and go into the bush. No trail, compass, or GPS, but Charlie knew where to go.

One of our adventures ended up at the Bark Lake Dam. What a dynamic spot. We had tramped through the bush for a couple of days, and looked uncommonly scruffy. Needed a shave and shower at least, but bedded down for the night anyway. Tent? Nah, we just had a canvas that we used for a 'lean-to'. Roughing it…you know. We had pitched our humble structure just off the trail about mid way down the artery to the foot of the Dam. It happened to be the only clearing around.

Break of dawn. Slowly we all get motivated begin cooking breakfast and just executing the early morning stuff. I'm the cook on this excursion and fried up some bacon, eggs and flapjacks. I was also responsible for bringing the plates. Unfortunately I left them at the base camp.

"Way to go." Charlie joked. "How the heck are we going to do this"? He laughed.

"Maybe we could all just eat out of the fry pan." I was grasping at straws.

"Ungh. Hang on a minute. I'll go down to the stream." Said Tabernac. "I'll bet there's some rocks that's pretty flat."

"Sure. Sounds good to me." Anything sounded more desirable than chowing down out of the greasy pan.

Three makeshift dishes soon appeared.

Now the amusement began. Here you have three rough looking guys that have been bushwhacking for a little too long…unshaven…not really clean…camped out under a tarp…feeding on bacon and eggs off of flat rocks. We likely appeared as a pack of desperate escaped convicts. While we were mawing down our grub, a troup of kayakers all dressed in trendy gear, (guaranteed to be worth a fortune not to mention the value of their kayaks) came strolling by our campsite. We looked like death reheated. Not one of them made any visual contact with us. We tried to be cordial but they didn't think that it was such a good idea. They just picked up their stride, eyes straight ahead and kept on their route. After our morning meal we went down to the base of the Dam where they were 'putting in' and explained why we looked like we did. Soon friends were made...so to speak.

Now why don't we talk about the ghost hunting? My mind wanders when I think of these times.

There is an old legend that some of the elders of this antiquated town pass on, the saga of the haunted "Crossroads." Yet mysteriously, no one admitted knowing its whereabouts. The story goes; that if you hesitated at this desolate intersection you'd be pelted with large rocks. The dense woods, thick with the tangled undergrowth were adjacent to the path often taken by the townsfolk. Stones would catapult out from nowhere. After you were dead your mangled body would be dragged to somewhere and devoured...never to be seen again, save for a few bones strewn here and there. Many unsuspecting travelers had vanished long ago. The older, superstitious seniors had advanced to intense fear. Their angst was genuine. It was evident by the look in their eyes whenever they spoke of the tabu.

"You boys look anxious to go." Aunt Rosie was on in her years but was as sharp as a tack.

"We're going to find the crossroads." Charlie dared...his wild stare gleaming. He knew well the pot that he was stirring. Word would get all over town of our antics by dusk.

Her eyes resembled copper pennies. "No! Stay here, it's nice here. Warm place to sleep. Why do you want to go to that terrible place? The devil is there," She growled. Her raspy voice was accumulating strength. "I'm very sure of that. Amy Polskis' father went there years back and was never heard from again."

She was desperately trying to convince us of the imminent danger that lurked in the underbrush. Charlie warned us of this, but we had to leave word with someone, where we were heading in the event that something did happen. We were going into some very grueling terrain. We assured her that there were no demons and that we would be fine. Off we pushed.

Now Charlie had some conception as to the location. It was on his grandfathers' land, which spanned hundreds of acres. He kind of knew where to go. The villager blocked it out of their memory, striving to forget. I had met these people in the past, but never ever heard anything about this lonely place. You'd have thought that it would have come up in some conversations at some story telling point in time. When we mentioned our task to his mom she presented the likely response that we got from Aunt Rosie.

"Roy! (Roy was his real name) You're not going there!" She was like a protective lioness. "Don't be crazy!"

Well we were bunked at the cabin at this time, finally showered and shaven. Charlie's mom roasted us up, such a spread. It was as though she was making our final farewell meal. She knew that she never had any mastery over (Roy), and just made the best of it. After all we were well into our thirties.

We packed up the van. I had this behemoth that would go through anything. Charlie's gathering the essentials and placing things meticulously into the back. "Fishing Rods."

"Check" I was the accredited list keeper, as I was so organized.

"Tackle"

"Check"

"Tent"

"Yup."

"Beer"

"How many are you packing?" I queried.

"One case each." That sounded like Charlie

"That's it?" I joked. "What if we get stranded?"

"That's right. Ok. I'll throw in an extra, just in case"

Off we went. That trail that we clumsily descended, (I wouldn't call it a road), was vicious. We had to pull up on the sides, for most of the time. The eroded ruts were more like craters that converted into streams. I have a better concept of how the Grand Canyon was shaped. We became hopelessly stuck several times just going in...and it's all down hill. Sheesh, are we ever getting out of this? How are we going to leave? There better not be anything down there.

"Hey Charlie...How're we getting out of here?"

"Don't worry" He insisted. "I know another way out. Think it's going to be better. Heh...Come on"

Tabernack was getting nervous. "Charlie, are you sure about this?"

"Naaaa...Come...on. Haaa...You guys worry too much"!

The road ended. It just ended. Right in the middle of nowhere. It didn't even go right...left...nowhere.

"I thought that there was another way out of here." Tabernack screeched jokingly.

"I did too." Said Charlie. "The road used to go off that way." Pointing to the left. "When I was a kid."

"When you were a kid? That was about a hundred years ago." I scolded.

"Yeah, I guess it was. Looks like it's kind of overgrown now. I guess that we should go scouting around for the crossroads. I know that it's somewhere around here." Charlie was getting a little more serious now.

We started walking along a path. Surely this was a well-traveled animal route to a pond or river or something. After about a half hour it kind of dwindled to nothing. There was a clearing though with only swaying grass bent in the soft breeze. The bush was behind us and off to either side. This void seemed to rush off in different directions, with stately oaks standing quietly and obediently like military troupes waiting for their command...all lined up on the edges.

"This is it!" Thundered Charlie. He was always theatrical and bigger than life.

"This is what?" I questioned.

"This is the crossroads! We're standing right in the middle. Look down there." Charlie pointed off to the left. "No trees down that way." Then pointed to the right. "Nothing that way."

He was right. The clearing, (if you want to call it that), we were following was the intersecting road. We found it. We thought that he was crazy at first, but here it was.

"Hey. Tabernac do you see it?" Charlie was getting excited.

"Yeah. You can see that the open area goes in four directions. It's got to be the place." Tabernac wanted as much as both of us, to realize the obvious that this was the place. Even if it wasn't…we were like kids determined to believe.

"Lets pitch the tent right here! Right in the middle of the road!"

We were having too much fun with this. We set up camp, lugged all of our gear, (Did I say gear or beer?), down the makeshift animal trail and prepared for the nightfall that was determined to arrive. We gathered up all of the firewood that we would need for the night…and then some. We didn't want to go wandering into the woods after dark.

The nighttime consumed us, all in a sudden. Man did it get black. You couldn't see your hand in front of your face.

It's a little later and by now we had gotten pretty well into the brew. We were laughing ecstatically at the foolishness of the superstitions, but still, way down deep we were a little on edge. The fire was roaring, and lit up the campsite well, but just look behind you and the abyss resembled a deep black curtain. The realization that someone or something could be lurking just a step away behind you made your skin crawl. The crackling of the fire sounding like twigs breaking under a foot, masked any noises that the beast may be making.

"COMMON!" Charlie bellowed. "HAAAA, WHERE ARE YOU! COME AND GET US!" He was like a wild man. Shouting at the top of his lungs.

We laughed, "Hey Charlie the only thing that you're going to attract is the police"

"Hah. How are they going to get in here?"

Tabernac agreed. "I don't even know how we got in here."

"You think that was hard. How are we ever getting out?" I said

"Naaah. Don't worry we'll get out. There's another way." The alcohol was doing its job.

The night came and went. Nothing happened. No ghosts. No mass murderers. No beasts (and this is bear country). Especially no rocks. We survived and still in one piece, save for a couple of hangovers. But we dealt with that effectively. A little tomato juice, bacon and eggs, toast and coffee. We'll be fine.

We packed up, and started back up the road. Charlies contingency exit was totally impassable. You couldn't even pretend that it was a trail. No choice. We had to scale back up the same way we belly flopped in. This road was all down hill coming in. So guess what. It's all uphill going out and we were getting trapped in the ruts when we came in.

"You've got to straddle the tracks. Stay up on the edge and middle." Charlie warned.

"Yup." I was concentrating on the difficult exercise ahead. This was no joke. The only way anyone would be rescuing us would be with a team of Clydesdales. Not even. I'm sure that a horse would be critically injured with this horrendous task.

"OH NO." Into the rut I slid. We were buried. We rocked it…back and forth…forth and back. It seemed hopeless.

"Rock it to the back and put the parking brake on." Charlie instructed.

"Ok, lets fill the ruts up with logs."

Off into the bush we went. We started dragging logs out the size of four by four posts and larger.

"Throw them into the ruts. Go ahead too. There are more…up a-ways in, and some are deeper."

Was this going to work? Charlie was a bushman and knew how to beat this kind of thing, so we just followed orders.

"Ok. Now give her hell." Charlie was strong willed and confident.

I climbed into the cockpit. Tabernac was in the back, and Charlie was riding shotgun. The engine roared. I poured the coals to her. WAAAAAAA! That big V8 was determined to tear us through this. Bouncing all over the place…I wouldn't let up. We were gaining ground. Charlie was right. We beat this first obstacle, nerves shattered but nonetheless unscathed. I heaved along, dodging the potholes and hollows. It was too much, I thought. Plodding through the muck, smashing on the rocks then somehow compromising the rushing stream that had washed out part of this maddening cart path. Now came the challenge. The vertical ascent was right in front of us. I knew it was there, because we had to come down it when we entered this hellhole. I stopped the van.

"How the hell are we going to climb that?" I was really panicked now. "Look at the size of those boulders. I don't remember them being that huge when we came in."

"Well, I guess that they were. You'll have to ride high on the edge. Watch you don't drop over the side, or we'll be screwed." Charlie wasn't big on losing hope. He was the 'just do it, and pay later' type of guy.

"I don't know if I can do it." I stammered. "Do you want to try it?" I looked at Tabernac.

"No way! You'd have to be crazy just to attempt this."

Charlie was always to the rescue whenever it was required. "I'll do it. Listen I'm going to have to let it all hang out."

"Charlie, do whatever you need to do. Even if you break something, what are we going to do, just stay here? Let her rip"

This is what he needed to hear. "We'll just walk on this stretch of the trail." Said Tabernac.

I agreed. Someone had to be alive to tell the tale.

Charlie mounted the beast. WAAAAAA. The engine wailed. Off she dashed. I thought it was going to flip right over. Bucking right…slamming down viciously on the brim of the boulder. Sparks shot out. Were we ever getting out of here? BRRRROOOONNN. The cries of the powerhouse fell on deaf ears. WWWAAA! Charlie was pulling out all the stops, gaining turf every effort. Just as he was seeing the apex the workhorse came to a halt. The tires were gyrating wildly. Smoke billowed from the right. She was hung up on a rock. The scent of a burnout filled the air. Precariously aimed at the edge of the bluff. The backup lights blared. A quick spurt to the rear. CRRHHUNK!…back in drive. SCCCCRREEEEEEEE!…heaving almost over the edge, she grabbed! Pulled Charlie to the summit.

WE CHEERED! "HEAAAAA…CHARLIE…YOU DID IT…WOOOO!"

"Of course I did. Did you ever doubt me? I told you we'd get out, no problem." Calm as could be.

"NO PROBLEM?" I barked.

He never let us live it down. It was the joke of the century. There's no doubt in my mind that a comparison to Charlie has never existed.

We moved out of town and had drifted apart over the years, but he called every Christmas to wish us a merry Christmas and Happy New Year. Never missed. Well Charlie passed away...died of cancer. He was the best friend a person could have. He used to say... "Everything is double. If you're nice to me," he'd beam, "I'll be twice as nice to you," and this was so true, "but if you're not nice to me...oooh you better watch out," he'd say with that devilish grin, "because you're getting it back double." God rest his soul.